Shi**y Limericks

Shi**y Limericks

#1 When It Comes To #2

ANTHONY GERBASIO

authorHOUSE®

AuthorHouse™
1663 Liberty Drive
Bloomington, IN 47403
www.authorhouse.com
Phone: 1-800-839-8640

Published by AuthorHouse   01/08/2013

ISBN: 978-1-4817-0530-1 (sc)
ISBN: 978-1-4817-0529-5 (e)

Library of Congress Control Number: 2013900297

I'd like to take this opportunity to say thanks to the people who, besides myself, helped make this book a reality. First, my wife Stephanie, who I love more than anything, and who first inspired me to put my silly ideas onto paper. She believed and supported me through the whole process from writing the limericks, bouncing ideas off of her and probably driving her insane in the process. To my awesome parents, Mom and Dad, you guys did a great job! Thanks for always getting my back! To the rest of my awesome family, thanks for always supporting my creativity and laughing at my jokes, even when my ideas were crazy and the jokes weren't funny (which was rare). To my friends, thanks for being the guinea pigs on which I tested my jokes and stories (and even inspiring some of them). A special thanks to Robb Vetter for keeping me on my game and forcing me to raise the bar. And a special thanks to Mike Kelly, one of my good friends, and definitely one of my favorite teachers, for helping me out with his linguistic skills (since creativity still needs to be grammatically correct).

Thanks to the readers as well for making my dream a reality, because without you, my book would sit on a shelf somewhere and gather dust.

I hope you all get as many laughs reading them as I got writing them!

Anthony Gerbasio

I wonder how I would do,
In a competition of poo.
'Cos it's always fun,
To be Number One,
Especially at Number Two!

I once overloaded on fruits.
It started to give me the toots.
But best to beware,
As I pollute the air.
For next I will shit on your boots.

Anthony Gerbasio

I went in to go take a pee,
But it turned out the joke was on me.
From the moment of starting,
I just kept on farting.
But the farts turned out to be 3-D.

Anthony Gerbasio

You know you can't take a chance,
When you're doing the poopie dance.
You have to drop "trou",
And you must do it now!
Or else you might shit in your pants!

I once was asleep in my room,
When suddenly there was a Boom!
It was such a loud fart,
I awoke with a start,
But the noise was much worse than the
fume!

If you are engaged in a clench,
Perhaps you could sit on a bench.
If your cheeks are too weak
You might spring a leak,
And then you'll be covered in stench.

Anthony Gerbasio

There once was a man from Nantucket,
Who took a big crap in a bucket.
'Twas smelly and soft,
And he threw it aloft.
But the passersby just couldn't duck it!

There once was a person at work,
Whom I thought to be quite a jerk.
His desk I crop-dusted,
But almost got busted,
Because of my big, guilty smirk!

Anthony Gerbasio

I had a bad case of the runs.
And these pants were my only ones.
But there wasn't a spill,
Thanks to the skill
And strength of my incredible buns!

One time while pooping at work,
I was a bit of a jerk.
For you see in my rush,
I neglected to flush.
And my reaction was only a smirk!

Anthony Gerbasio

There once was a man they called "Tater",
He had to use a respirator.
With farts so robust,
He felt that he must
Be getting "Force-choked" by Darth
Vader!

I wanted to swim in the pool,
The water was so clear and cool.
But as I climbed the ladder
I felt something splatter,
And looked like a pants-shitting fool!

Anthony Gerbasio

There once was a man named Abe Lincoln.
Who sat on his toilet while thinkin':
"I've mended the nation,
And earned admiration"
But meanwhile the bathroom was stinkin'!

All of us men should be wary,
'Cos pooping can be kind of scary.
This might sound "icky",
But you will get sticky
If your ass is a little too hairy!

Anthony Gerbasio

I once had to take a huge crap.
I thought I'd be done in a snap.
But I sat and I squeezed,
And leaned on my knees,
And soon I could not feel my lap!

A boy asked a girl to a dance,
She smiled and gave him a chance.
But his moment of happiness
Turned into crappiness
When he sharted and ruined his pants!

Anthony Gerbasio

The girl had accepted the date,
But told the boy he had to wait.
For you see at the dance,
She too shit her pants.
With that they each found their soul
mate.

I ate a head of cauliflower,
I thought it would give me some power.
It did, but alas,
The power was gas,
And I had it for over an hour.

Anthony Gerbasio

There once was a man with a slinky,
Who was feeling a little bit kinky.
I can't put into words,
What it did to his turds,
They're shaped weird but still just as
stinky!

One day in my car on the road,
I felt like I had to explode.
I pulled off to the side,
And my dignity died
As I made the bike lane my commode!

Anthony Gerbasio

One day I couldn't avoid
My wife who was very annoyed.
For the food from the deli
Declared war on my belly,
And the bathroom had gotten destroyed.

I once had to go change a diaper.
It couldn't have been any riper.
But the baby just giggled
And awkwardly wiggled
And made it a challenge to wipe her.

Anthony Gerbasio

Whether a knight in full armor,
Or even a potato farmer.
We all have to poop,
You know that's the scoop.
From the President to a snake charmer.

A man said to his nagging wife:
"My darling, I'll love you for life . . .
Just leave me alone
When I sit on the throne!"
As the smell of his movement was rife!

Anthony Gerbasio

I'd done my best to ensure
The house didn't smell like manure.
The windows were open
And I was just hopin'
My stomach would soon have a cure.

Here's a story that's silly
About my friend who's named Billy.
There was no solution
To the air pollution
Caused by his four bowls of chili!

Anthony Gerbasio

Some friends had decided to prank
Their coworker down at the bank.
They put some Ex-Lax
In some of his snacks
And the bathroom soon filled with his
stank!

There once was a man from Nebraska,
That was on his way to Alaska.
But he got his poop on
Way up in the Yukon
And stopped one time to play Canasta.

Anthony Gerbasio

A brave knight said to his young squire
As they sat by the camp fire
"Finish your soup
And then go clean the poop
From my armor that you so admire".

Be careful when you're at the zoo.
The monkeys all like to throw poo!
For as you walk by
They'll make a shit pie
And throw all that shit right at you!

Anthony Gerbasio

There once was a magic poop gnome.
Around the whole world he would roam.
And he would retrieve
All the turds that you leave
In the bathroom inside of your home!

I sat on a plane in first class,
When soon I was stricken with gas.
That's not the whole story,
For in the lavatory
I blew up the plane with my ass!

Anthony Gerbasio

I took a vacation to France.
And there was a tour guide named Lance.
But he had a stench
Undeniably French
That seemed to exude from his pants!

A husband and wife set up camp.
The wife had soon suffered a cramp.
'Twas no toilet tissue
But it wasn't an issue.
She wiped with some leaves like a champ!

Anthony Gerbasio

'Twas at my high school graduation
I witnessed a fool's defecation.
He soiled his pants
At Pomp and Circumstance
And ruined the whole celebration!

My friend and I went scuba diving.
But he had the runs when arriving.
Our time was so grand
I stuck out my hand
But he shit himself while high–fiving!

Anthony Gerbasio

I once had a bad stomachache
I had no antacid to take
I farted and sighed,
My wife nearly died
So I sprayed some Febreeze for her sake!

The bathroom was locked so I waited.
"Hurry up in there" I stated.
The door opened quickly
The man had looked sickly
It turns out he'd been constipated!

Anthony Gerbasio

Our cat liked to poop on the floor
My wife couldn't take anymore
He wouldn't obey
So water she sprayed
And he learned his lesson for sure!

After a long night of drinking
My morning dump sure would be stinking
With every new beer
My head was less clear
Man, what the hell was I thinking?

Anthony Gerbasio

States